TONY JOHNSTON

Once in the Country

POEMS OF A FARM

ILLUSTRATED BY

THOMAS B. ALLEN

G. P. PUTNAM'S SONS — NEW YORK

Remembering the Santa Ysabel Ranch,
the Richfield station
and Susan Hertel—T. J.

To the renaissance
of the family farm.—T. B. A.

Text copyright © 1996 by Tony Johnston. Illustrations copyright © 1996 by Thomas B. Allen
All rights reserved. This book, or parts thereof, may not be reproduced in any form without
permission in writing from the publisher. G. P. Putnam's Sons, a division of The Putnam & Grosset Group,
200 Madison Avenue, New York, NY 10016. G. P. Putnam's Sons, Reg. U.S. Pat. & Tm. Off.
Published simultaneously in Canada. Printed in Hong Kong by South China Printing Co. (1988) Ltd.
Book designed by Gunta Alexander. Text set in Garamond #3
The art was done with pastels on Canson paper.
Library of Congress Cataloging-in-Publication Data
Johnston, Tony,   Once in the country / by Tony Johnston; illustrated by Thomas B. Allen.   p.   cm.
Summary: A collection of poems depicting life in the country throughout the seasons of the year.
1. Country life—Juvenile poetry. 2. Nature—Juvenile poetry. 3. Children's poetry, American.
[1. Country life—Poetry. 2. Seasons—Poetry. 3. American poetry.]   I. Allen, Thomas B. (Thomas Burt),
1928- ill. II. Title. PS3560.0393053 1996 811'.54—dc20 94-40899 CIP AC
ISBN 0-399-22644-3   10 9 8 7 6 5 4 3 2 1   First Impression

Contents

Once in the Country

Once beside a pool
I held a snakeskin to the light.

Once in summer sun
I gave a dead tree one good kick.

Once where it was cool
I watched a beetle curl up tight.

Once just for the fun
I gave a salt block one good lick.

Once in wet, grey light
I heard a frog sing in the rain.

Once upon a hill
I found a shiny, perfect stone.

Once when it was night
I heard a mouse eat stolen grain.

Once when I was still
I saw a spotted calf be born.

Milking

The moon is up
but day is on the rise.

Half-asleep I set
my wobbly stool,
pat our big Holstein
and begin to pull
milk down
from her warm-glove udder.

Soon I close my eyes
(keeping the milking rhythm)
and listen
to the barn—

One last cricket (hidden)
trilling away,
old boards creaking,
chickens speaking their foreign tongue,
grunting of a sleeping sow,
sweep of the cow's long tail,
warm milk stinging
the inside of
my pail.

Promises From sweet straw hollows
I gather eggs,
still warm from the bodies
of settled hens.

I place them in my basket.
Gently, so gently.
Each one is
a promise.

The Nest   I found a nest of speckled quail
Beneath a speckled bush somewhere.
I made no sound. I breathed no breath.
I went away and left it there.

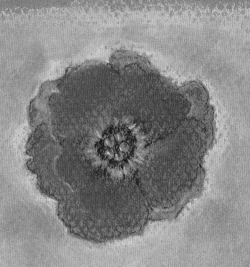

Cows
Where the old barn
slumps in the sun,
they browse for clumps
of poppies
between the spokes of a broken
wheel,
then slow as summer
wander
down to the fence
and stretch to reach
lavender lupine.

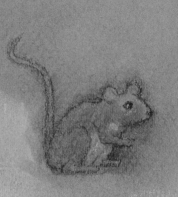

Goodnight Come evening, in the fading light,
I go to the barn to say goodnight—
To the plow horse chewing in his stall,
To a brown mouse hiding in the wall,
To pigeons cooing out of sight,
To little bats in velvet flight.
I whisper, quiet as I can,
To the quiet lump of sleeping lambs.

My Overalls   The best thing is their color,
       old-night or early-dawn.

No, the best thing is their limpness
       when I hoist them on.

No, the best thing is their looseness
       like the soft skin of a pup.

No, the best thing is their buckles
       like a suitcase snapping shut.

No, the best thing is their perfume
       of cows and hay and dung.

No, the best thing is their many holes
       to let in all the sun.

My Mule Lolly

Through the dry field Lolly goes
plowing up the rippling rows.

All day long she strains and toils
scratching at the bone-hard soil.

All day long, up and back.
Lolly leads. I walk her track.

We plow our plot, old Lol and I.
A red-tailed hawk plows up the sky.

Turtle   From my secret swimming hole
I see only water.
And trees. And sky.
Then I spy
two yellow eyes
and a dark mound
stroking, gliding by.
He snaps at a dragonfly
and goes on.
Pays me no mind.
The day is fine. Summer weather.
So we just keep stroking along
together.

Skipping Stones

The small stones
    skim
the pond
dipping
    low
now and then
to play the water
like a green
    banjo
running lightly
    along
its strings
plucking out
an
    old
        wet
           song.

Grandma
For F.K.H.

In the small kitchen, warm with cooking,
I wrap my arms around her,
burrowing close,
like I burrow into my pillow,
smelling the singe
of old starch in her apron,
her good perfume—
of onions and vanilla.

Shep   Once he ran the huddled hills,
dizzy with each smell, and flushed
hidden quail
          —his only joy.
Good old dog. Good old boy.

Now he sighs, too slow to rush,
dozing on the porch, and dreams
hidden quail
          —his only joy.
Good old dog. Good old boy.

The Owner

As day dwindles to stars
the skunk comes strutting
across the road
and climbs the sagging cabin steps,
stopping now—again—
to sniff the wind.
He swaggers through the door,
explores old jelly jars
spider-webbed with ragged lace,
tastes a photograph grown dim, then
curls up on a mattress,
striped like him.

Fence   As light as leaves
the last birds
take flight,
leaving a fence
of song
strung around
the field.

White Cat Winter   White cat Winter
                           prowls
                           the farm,
                           tiptoes
                           soft
                           through withered corn,
                           creeps
                           along low walls
                           of stone,
                           falls asleep
                           beside
                           the barn.

Poor   Scarecrow shivers in
his thin silver shirt beneath
the November moon.

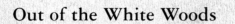

Out of the White Woods   Out of the white woods
a deer steps lightly onto
the road. Our eyes meet.

So Many Horses

For C.W.H.

At sundown the old man stands alone
and thinks of the horses, dead and gone,
that plodded the road with loads of hay
and worked their lives out day on day.

So many horses, so many years.
He smells their sweat and faintly hears
the ghostly blow of their patient breath
upon his sleeve. He feels them snuff

and gently nuzzle gifts of grain
cupped in the hollow of his hand.
So many horses, dead so long,
he leads in dreams as night comes on.